OF **BRAINS** & BEAUTY

A FATHER-DAUGHTER JOURNEY
AMONG THE EXTRAORDINARY

WRITTEN BY
ROBERTO NOCE

ILLUSTRATED BY
CATHY DOUGHERTY

OF BRAINS & BEAUTY
A FATHER-DAUGHTER JOURNEY AMONG THE EXTRAORDINARY

Illustrations by Cathy Dougherty

Design & Layout by Jacob Bascle

First printing, 2014.

DEDICATION

To my daughter Francesca:
Your passion for life, hunger for
adventure, and thirst for learning
continues to inspire me.

Let us respect childhood;
let us honor the soul
of that small creature of God
who can already make choices of the best
if we take the time to awaken her reason
and make her use her judgment.

-St. Madeleine Sophie Barat

AUTHOR'S INTRODUCTION

Right before bed-time, when all is quiet, dad reads to his daughter a story every night, and from the magical world of imagination, real characters and places come to life, one at a time, chapter after chapter.

Storytelling is an amazing tool. It brings adults and children together and enriches the often limited family time by creating a moment and a place in time were we can meet anyone and travel anywhere.

I have written this book for parents, grandparents, and teachers to share with children true facts about individuals in history with brilliant minds and places that are truly magnificent in their inspirational power. In each of the nine chapters of the book the reader is guided by a different historical character through his or her own life and to familiar places. The stories are written for kids between 9 and 11 years of age, but older kids and adults will enjoy them too.

While the list covers only a handful of great people and places, there are many more that deserve consideration for their brilliant minds and contributions to mankind or for their magnificent beauty. It is my sincere wish that this book will represent an opportunity for sharing special moments with your children and incite you to continue a voyage of discovery and true learning that shall have no boundaries.

TABLE of CONTENTS

INTRODUCTION

Lola always looked forward to the first Saturday of each month. That's when she and her dad would get up extra early and head over to the outdoor flea market on the old amusement park grounds. It was their special together-time and Lola really enjoyed spending the morning with her dad. The day would start with a fresh coffee for dad and a strawberry smoothie for Lola. Hand in hand, they would stroll through the market place looking through all the vendor's wares in search of just the right "treasure."

"The early bird gets the worm," Dad would say, as he sorted through table after table. Anything and everything can be found at a flea market, and all the bargain hunters knew to get there early, or else miss out on a great find. The vendor tables held everything from antique jewelry, to classic comics, to collectible toys, and more.

Often, the same vendors would return every month and the prospect of fabulous bargains made those early morning outings so worthwhile!

One bright and sunny Saturday, Lola headed for her favorite vendor table only to discover a new seller in that spot. Instead of finding jewelry, she discovered a table laden with books of every shape and size. Behind the table stood a cheerful woman with a kindly smile. Reaching behind a large stack, she brought out a book and said, "Do you like to read? When my daughter was your age, I read this book to her every night."

Lola took the proffered book and examined the cover: *Of Brains and Beauty*.

Interesting title, she thought.

"It's a very special book," declared the woman, with a twinkle in her eye. "When you open the pages and begin to read, the people and places will come alive—and learning will be so much fun for you!"

"That sounds wonderful!" said Dad as he approached the table. Lola loved a good story and couldn't wait to open the book.

"Can we read this together, Dad, please? Every night, OK?"

"Absolutely," he replied. "We'll start tonight!"

And so the adventures began...

Wolfgang Amadeus Mozart

"Neither a lofty degree of intelligence nor imagination nor both together go to the making of genius. Love, love, love, that is the soul of genius."

"So, how was school today?" asked Dad.

"We had Music class this morning. It was pretty fun," replied Lola. "We listened to classical music by Mozart and I really liked the class."

"I'm glad your teacher introduced you to Mozart's music. He's one of my favorite composers," Dad said. "Would you like to learn more about him? Let's see what our special book has to say about Wolfgang Amadeus Mozart, shall we?"

As Dad started reading aloud, Lola began to picture Mozart in her mind. She imagined him as a young man, dressed in the fashion of the late eighteenth century, wearing a white wig and knee length breeches and shoes with fancy buckles. The image took form.

"What would Mozart most like for us to know?" wondered Dad. "If he were here right now, Lola, what do you think he would tell us about himself?"

"I can answer that question for you." Lola and her dad were startled. Where had that voice come from? Looking up from the book, they saw a surprise. Before them stood Wolfgang Amadeus Mozart himself—just as the woman from the flea market had predicted!

"This is gonna be cool," thought Lola.

"Wow!" said Dad. "This is amazing! Please tell us about yourself Mr. Mozart."

"I would begin by saying that music was my life," replied Mozart. "I was born into a musical family. My older sister played the piano, and my father was a successful composer, violinist, and assistant concert master at the court of Salzburg in the European country of Austria. In 1759, when I was only 4 years old, my father began my formal lessons on the keyboard. At age 5, I wrote my first composition that premiered in Salzburg—and I became known as a *child prodigy,* a status my family was very proud of!"

"Just like I'm very proud of my daughter," thought Dad.

"At age 6," Mozart continued, "I performed for the Empress Maria Theresa and her family at Schoenbrunn Palace which launched my career as a pianist and composer. That performance led to many tours throughout Europe. My sister and I played for the royal courts in England, France, Poland, Italy, and Austria."

"Was it fun to travel? Did you ever get bored with performing? Were you famous? Did you enjoy writing music?" Lola had so many questions!

Mozart was thoughtful for a moment, then he replied. "I loved writing music, Lola. Music truly was my passion! Although I only lived to be 35, I wrote and performed hundreds of symphonies, concertos, sonatas, and operas. It was not always an easy life though. You see, back in my time cities like Prague, Vienna, and Salzburg were controlled by the aristocracy—who had money and power. They would commission artists and musicians to entertain their courts, and often paid very well. However, we sometimes had to wait months for invitations and payments from them.

"To answer another of your questions....yes, I enjoyed visiting different cities and palaces. I even learned to speak 15 languages! But travel at that time was very difficult and, by today's standards, very primitive. No fast food places to be sure!

Mozart smiled. "I never tired of performing and composing. I would compose entire symphonies and create all the parts for the instruments in my head. I imagined all the sounds without hitting a single key or playing a single note. When I first moved to Vienna as a young man, I supported myself through teaching, writing music, and playing in concerts. Vienna is also where I met and married my wife, Constanze. We had six children, but sadly, only two survived. Our sons, Karl Thomas and Franz Xaver, brought us much joy! During this period, in Vienna, my music flourished and I was able to provide my family with a lavish lifestyle. For a time, we were quite well-to-do. We lived in an exclusive apartment building, kept servants, and had a wonderful social life.

"However, our fortunes sometimes went up and down depending on what was happening in the world," Mozart explained. "For example, when Austria was at war, during the late 1780s, the noble families couldn't afford to support musicians and the arts declined. Those were difficult times financially, but when the war ended our circumstances improved again and I was able to compose some of my most admired work."

"I really enjoyed listening to your music in class today, Mr. Mozart," said Lola. "I can't wait to hear more someday!"

"I applaud teachers like yours who make it exciting to learn about me and other musicians. It's wonderful to know that future generations continue to enjoy my music," Mozart said with glee. "That makes me very happy! Never stop learning and having fun doing so!"

The Schönbrunn Palace

Lola and her dad were enthralled by Mozart's story. Being able to listen to Wolfgang Amadeus Mozart describe his life in his own words was simply amazing!

"You traveled all over Europe performing for Kings, Queens, Emperors, and Empresses, Mr. Mozart," Lola enquired. "I'm curious—did you have a favorite place to visit? Dad and I would really like to hear about that and about what made it so special."

"I'm glad you asked," replied Mozart. "I would like to tell you about a place that is very dear to me: The Schönbrunn Palace, where I had my musical debut performing for the Austrian Empress Maria Theresa. The Palace is located in Vienna, the capital of the European country of Austria. It is a place of fabulous beauty and was the summer residence of the Imperial Family. The vast estate encompasses 435 acres - that's almost equivalent to 435 football fields! In fact, the grounds are so extensive it would take you most of a day to visit the magnificent palace and gardens. And we mustn't forget the zoo! Schönbrunn is home to the oldest zoo of its kind in the world."

"I love zoos!" exclaimed Lola. "Did they really have a zoo way back then? Being on the royal estate, was the zoo only for wealthy people to enjoy?"

"Tiergarten Schönbrunn (German for Schönbrunn Zoo) dates back to 1752 when Austrian Emperor Maximilian II started keeping exotic animals on the palace grounds," explained Mozart. "So, yes, the zoo was originally a collection enjoyed only by the emperor, his family, and guests. However, it was later opened to the public and can still be visited today. Tiergarten Schönbrunn is now among the most modern zoos in the world and their motto 'Schoenbrunn should be a zoo of happy animals,' is visibly posted everywhere. Over the centuries visitors witnessed the arrival of the first giraffe, the birth of the first elephant in captivity, and the very rare giant pandas.

"Naturally, no tour of Schönbrunn would be complete without a visit to the park. There you will be amazed by the orangery, where my music is now performed in grand style almost every day. The orangery was created as a green house, with an innovative floor heating system designed to ensure the proper temperature for the citrus trees and potted plants. Being the only heated building on the estate, many winter parties were held there by the imperial family."

Mozart continued, "Also in the park is an amazing steel and glass construction known as the Palmenhaus (palm house) which houses a number of exotic plants from different climates. One of the more unusual sites in the park is the mock Roman Ruin, a gorgeous landscape and water architectural display.

Such a display was all the rage at the time and served as a romantic background for theater productions. Other unique creations in the park include obelisks, a maze, a Japanese garden, a Botanic garden, and the Neptune fountain."

"And back to the Palace, what about the Palace itself...what was it like?" asked Lola.

"Ah, the Palace...I do recall a legend from long ago," replied Mozart. "In 1569, the site was known as Kattenburg and was a hunting lodge for Emperor Maximilian. Stories say that Maximilian's son, Emperor Matthias, discovered a beautiful spring while hunting there. He is said to have exclaimed, 'So ein schoner Brunnen,' which means 'what a beautiful spring' and led to the name Schönbrunn.

"Later, the hunting lodge was destroyed by the Turkish. Emperor Leopold I then commissioned a great court architect, Johann Bernhard Fischer von Erlach, to construct a palace grander than Versailles." Mozart continued, "Versailles is a palace outside of Paris, France, and its magnificent formal gardens became the ultimate model for palaces in Europe. Unfortunately, due to war, the original plans were too expensive and Emperor Leopold I settled for a less complex, yet still fabulous, design."

"Did it take long to build the palace?" asked Dad. "I know technology was very different back then. The builders wouldn't have had the equipment we have now."

"You are correct, sir," replied Mozart. "Construction began in 1696 but was only completed in the mid eighteenth century during the reign of Empress Maria Theresa.

"At one time, as many as 1,000 people lived in the 1,441 rooms and halls of the complex. One of the most remarkable chambers in the palace is the round Chinese cabinet, an entire room decorated with porcelain. This room is where Empress Maria Theresa held meetings with advisors." Mozart smiled. "Of course, *my* favorite room in the palace is the Spiegelsaal (Mirror Hall) where my sister and I first performed for the Empress."

"Well, we can certainly understand why Schönbrunn is so special," said Dad. "Thanks for joining us tonight!"

Dr. Sally Ride

"All adventures, especially into new territory, are scary."

Lola and her Dad were settling down for their special night-time routine. They both enjoyed sharing their day with each other, followed by a chapter from their favorite new book.

"What was the best part of your day today?" asked Dad.

"Science class! Science is my favorite subject!" declared Lola. "Today we studied the solar system and space exploration. When I grow up, I want to be an astronaut just like Sally Ride!"

"Lola, if you study hard you can be anything you want," said Dad with a smile. "My daughter the astronaut. I like the sound of that! Ever wondered what it would be like to explore space?"

"Let's check the book, Dad. There's a chapter about Sally Ride," said Lola. Dad flipped through the pages.

"Here it is!" He began to read aloud. "Sally Ride was born on May 26, 1951. She grew up in Los Angeles, California and went to Stanford University"

"Where I majored in physics, and English," finished Sally Ride. It had happened again! Lola was thrilled! The person she was so interested in learning about was now standing before her.

Dad smiled and said, "Welcome Dr. Ride! Please continue."

"Once I completed my studies and earned a PhD in physics, I saw NASA's advertisement for astronauts. I read the qualifications and said, 'I'm one of those people'. I applied, and made the cut and joined NASA, the National Aeronautics and Space Administration astronaut program. That was back in 1982."

"That was a pretty big deal at the time, wasn't it?" asked Dad.

"It sure was," replied Sally. "Thousands of candidates wanted to be part of the space program, and no woman had ever been selected to be an astronaut before."

"We learned about you in school today," said Lola. "You became the first American woman and the youngest person in space! What was that like?"

"It wasn't easy, Lola, but I was determined. The astronaut program was very rigorous and I worked really hard. I managed to earn a spot aboard the space shuttle Challenger as a mission specialist. We launched from the Kennedy

Space Center in Florida on June 18, 1983 and returned to earth on June 24th. There were five crew members on that mission: four men and one woman—me!

"I subsequently performed as an on-orbit Capsule Communicator, or CAPCOM, on two other missions. A CAPCOM helps bridge the communication between the ground control and the Flight Control Team. As an astronaut, I was well suited for that job."

"Was it difficult being the only female astronaut?" asked Dad.

"Of course, it took time for a woman to be accepted as an equal in an era when the sciences were still predominantly run by men. At first, people would ask me such questions as: Would I wear make-up in space? Will I cry on the job? How will I use the toilet in space? One famous comedian even made a joke that the shuttle would be delayed because I needed to find a purse to match my shoes!

"Those comments seem pretty silly now," continued Sally, "but that is how things were back then. I proved that a woman could do the job as well as any man. I trained to parachute from a plane, to survive at sea and the acceleration of rocket launches, and to float weightless. I learned to fly a jet! I helped develop the robotic arm for the space shuttle, which is like the space shuttle's right hand. It moves objects around with an incredibly delicate touch. That made me a deserving equal on the shuttle crew. It was the most amazing experience! "

"By the way, Lola" said Dr. Sally "do you know how you eat a sandwich in space?"

"No?" said both Lola and Dad, leaning forward.

"Fast, before it floats away!" she explained. They all had a laugh at that.

"I enjoyed playing football with the neighborhood boys and I was a great tennis player but I chose college and science instead. Since I was a little girl all I wanted to do was fly, soar into space, look around at the heavens and back at Earth. Later on I gave back, and worked at making science and engineering cool again for young people, especially girls."

"Thank you for sharing your dream-come-true story with us, Dr. Ride!" Lola enthused. "I'm going to do my best to study hard so I can keep being a good student and make a difference in people's lives someday, perhaps becoming an astronaut too."

"I'm so happy to hear that, Lola! I'm very proud to be a role model for all children. My hope is that boys and girls will be inspired to reach for the stars!"

The Moon

Lola and her Dad were very impressed with all that Sally Ride had accomplished in her lifetime.

"As I mentioned before, I've always been fascinated with the moon," continued Sally.

"Me too!" said Lola. "Last year we moved to a new home in the country and, in the evenings, after I have finished all of my homework, I love to sit on the porch outside with dad and look at the night sky—once, I even saw a shooting star!"

"I remember that night, Lola," said Dad. "We were gazing at the second full moon that month, which we had never noticed before. Can you tell us about the moon, Dr. Ride?"

"I'd love to! And back to what you were saying, the second full moon in a month is called a "blue moon". It happens infrequently. That is why we have the expression "once in a Blue Moon", which refers to a rare event.

"The moon is the easiest celestial object for us to find in the night sky because it is the most luminous object in the sky after the sun. The moon is also the only celestial body other than earth on which humans have ever set foot. It takes 27.3 days for the moon to rotate on its axis *and* to orbit the Earth. That means the moon is always showing us the same face. But, the moon doesn't have its own light source—we see the moon because the light of the sun is reflected off its surface.

"There are numerous theories about how the moon was created," Sally continued, "but recent evidence indicates it formed when an enormous collision with another celestial object broke a chunk of Earth away. We believe the moon is over 4.5 billion years old!"

"How far away is the moon? How big is it really?" Lola asked.

"Good questions!" replied Sally. "Have you noticed that sometimes the moon looks large, and other times looks really small in the sky? That's because the moon takes an elliptical path around the earth - which means the moon can get closer to the earth and then can get farther. At its closest point, known as the perigee, the moon is only 225,622 miles away. But at its most distant point, called the apogee, the moon is as far away as 406,696 miles from earth. Scientists calculate the average distance, known as the semi-major axis, to be 238,855 miles. Here's another cool fact for you: The moon is 1/4 the size of earth, which makes the moon's gravity much less than earth's gravity."

"Do you know what gravity is?" asked Sally. Lola thought gravity had something to do with weight, but she wasn't sure about that. "You are on the right track," encouraged Sally.

"Let's see if I can explain it for you...there are two important facts about gravity. First, we know that gravity is a force that pulls all objects towards each other. Second, the greater the mass of an object, the stronger the pull of its gravity. In other words, a body with greater mass will pull stronger than a body with smaller mass. So, for example Earth, much bigger than anything on its surface, pulls us toward the center of the Earth and keeps us, air, and anything around us from drifting off into space. Gravity also causes things to fall to the ground."

"So, that means 'weight' is equal to the strength of the gravitational pull between two objects?" Dad asked. "And if the moon is smaller than the earth, then I would weigh a lot less on the moon. Haha! So Lola, if you weighed 100 pounds here, you would only weigh 16.6 pounds on the moon." He glanced at Lola, "You would certainly be able to jump really high!" he said with a wink.

"By the way, have you noticed those bumps on the surface of the moon? Over the years asteroids have collided against the moon's rocky surface and left it covered in craters. Want to know one more really neat thing about the moon? The atmosphere!" said Sally. "The moon has an atmosphere composed of very, very thin gases. There is no air to breathe, so there is no wind to blow flags. That means that a layer of dust can remain undisturbed for hundreds of years. The prints from the first moon landing are still there, Lola."

"You were an astronaut, Dr. Ride. Did you ever visit the moon?" asked Lola.

"I wish I could have," sighed Sally, "but I *was* fortunate enough to be part of two shuttle missions that gave me the opportunity to be in space. I was so passionate about the moon that in 1987, I led a team that wrote a report recommending that NASA develop a base there where people could do research, learn, and work. Maybe you'll have that opportunity someday when you become an astronaut Lola."

"Thanks for visiting us this evening, Dr. Ride. Do you have any final words of advice for my future astronaut?" asked Dad.

"I certainly do! Remember, Lola, "*All adventures, especially into new territory, are scary,*' so if you have a dream and are passionate about it don't be scared to chase it and always reach for the stars!"

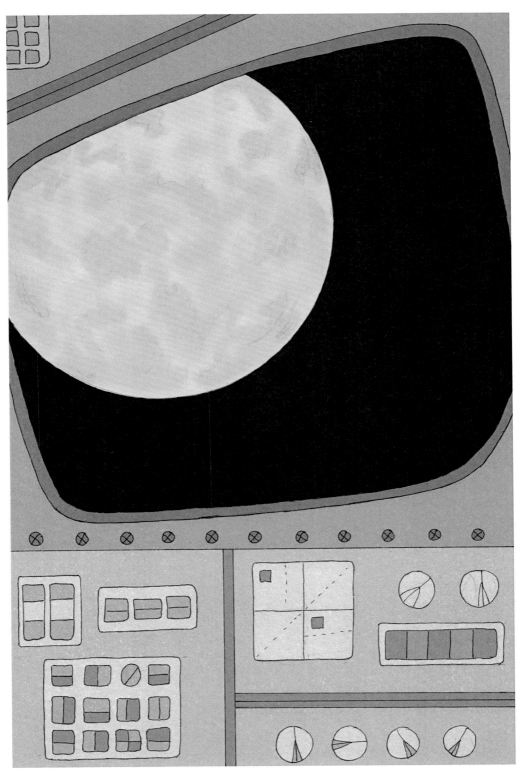

Galileo Galilei

"You cannot teach a man anything; you can only help him discover it himself."

Lola had spent most of the evening viewing the heavens through her telescope. The moon and the constellations were awesome.

"The sky was so beautiful tonight," sighed Lola. "I wish we could have stayed outside longer."

"It's a school night, so no more star-gazing for now," said Dad. "We can spend some more time together tomorrow night. I enjoy using the telescope as much as you do, but now it's time to call it a day."

Dad and Lola sat on their comfy armchair, picked up their favorite book, and settled down to read.

"This chapter should interest you, Lola. Do you know who else had a passion for the stars? I'll give you a hint: this person is sometimes called 'The Father of Modern Science.'"

"Why, sir, you must be speaking of me!" a deep voice replied. An image materialized—the voice belonged to a stately gentleman, dressed in the garb of the late 1500's.

"I know who you are!" cried Lola excitedly. "You're Galileo Galilei, the astronomer! I recognize you from the picture in my science book."

"Nice to meet you Mr. Galilei," said Dad. "We're glad you are here. Can you please tell us about your life?"

"Please, call me Galileo," replied their guest. "I was born in 1564 in Pisa, which is in the Italian region of Tuscany." Continued the gentleman, "My father, Vincenzo Galilei, was a famous musician and he wanted me to become a doctor. But while at medical school at the University of Pisa, I discovered that my passion was for mathematics. So I dropped medicine and became a tutor, then a professor of mathematics."

"You wore many hats in your lifetime, and discovered many more things, didn't you?" asked Dad. "Astronomer, philosopher, physicist and mathematician, right?"

"You are correct, Sir" said Galileo. "It all started in 1609 when I came across the 'spyglass'—a device built by Dutch eyeglass makers, which made distant objects appear closer. Mathematics helped me improve upon it and build the 'telescope', which was also designed to look at distant objects but was a more powerful instrument than the spyglass. With the telescope, I gazed into the heavens and made my first discovery. I saw that the moon was not a smooth sphere but had mountains and craters! I also discovered that Jupiter had its own revolving moons, and that Venus had phases like the moon. I studied the planet Saturn, and discovered sunspots.

"However, my passion got me in trouble too. Most people in my time believed that the Earth was at the center of the universe and that the Sun and planets revolved around it. My gazing made me believe that it was the other way around: Earth and all other planets revolve around the Sun. Because of this, at the age of 69, I was sentenced to life imprisonment in my home."

Galileo continued, "Throughout my entire life I never stopped learning, Lola! I was fascinated by so many things that you would take for granted now. I was especially passionate about my studies on objects in motion.

"And that interest lead to another of my important discoveries. While a mathematics professor at the University of Pisa," said Galileo "the belief at that time was that heavier objects fell at a faster rate than light ones. I disagreed and performed an experiment. I went up the Tower of Pisa and from the top of the tower, I dropped cannon balls of the same material, but different weights. They landed at the same time. That proved my theory of falling bodies: all falling objects (light or heavy) fall at the same rate of speed!"

"What else?" asked Lola. She was passionate about learning, too!

"Ok, one more," smiled Galileo. "Perhaps you have heard of my discovery called 'The Law of the Pendulum'?"

Lola and Dad shook their heads.

Galileo explained, "I always tried to be observant of the world around me, and one day in 1581, I was walking through the church in Pisa. Deep in thought, I glanced up and noticed a swinging chandelier. The breeze made the chandelier swing in larger and smaller arcs. When I returned home, I experimented with two pendulums of equal length and swung one with a large sweep and the other with a small sweep. Can you guess what I discovered?"

"I know! I know!" Lola enthused. "Even though they had different size sweeps, they kept time together."

"You are quite right, young lady," replied Galileo. "That discovery became the base for modern clocks."

"And speaking of clocks," said Dad ruefully, "Look at the time—it's gotten pretty late! Thanks so much for the lesson this evening. We've really enjoyed your story."

"Good night, dear Lola," added Galileo. "And remember: love the stars fondly and you will never be fearful of the night."

The Leaning Tower of Pisa

Galileo was a fascinating guest, and Lola especially enjoyed how his love for learning, confidence in his own beliefs, and overall genius brought so much contribution to science and mankind.

"Before I take my leave, there is one more thing I would like to share with you," said Galileo. "It is a monument, which is very special and dear to me: The Leaning Tower of Pisa. The Leaning Tower of Pisa was the place where I performed my experiments with falling objects."

"I've heard of Pisa," commented Dad. "What makes that particular tower so special?"

"I was born in Pisa," Galileo replied. "It is a beautiful place steeped in history, and one of the largest cities in Tuscany, Italy. The city is the home of the University of Pisa, which dates back to the 12th century. There are many ancient churches, palaces, and beautiful bridges across the River Arno. To most, however, Pisa is famous for housing the incredible leaning tower.

"The city began as a simple seaport. Over the years, it became a very powerful city-state and flourished commercially and militarily during the Middle Ages. Numerous victories brought a great deal of wealth to Pisa. The proud citizens decided to show the world how important their city was by building a great cathedral complex," Galileo explained.

"The plan included a cathedral (Duomo), a baptistery, a cemetery, and a bell tower (campanile). The complex was named Piazza dei Miracoli, the Square of Miracles. The square is a walled area that lies in the center of Pisa with partly paved and partly grassy areas. People often confuse the square's name with "campo dei miracoli", which, you may recall, is a magical field in the book *Pinocchio*. Piazza dei Miracoli with its famous buildings is a stunning sight, a true testament to the genius and capabilities of man.

"The bell tower was the third and final structure built for the project. Called 'the Tower of Pisa', it has a cylindrical body made of stone, which is surrounded by open galleries with arches and pillars on the bottom and a belfry on the top. The bells were all tuned to musical scales. The tower today stands at approximately 191 feet tall and 64 feet round at the foundation. Construction began in 1173, but wasn't completed until 1399—over two hundred years later!"

"That's crazy!" exclaimed Lola. "How could it possibly take so long to finish? There must have been some serious building problems!"

"Precisely, young lady!" Galileo replied. "Only three of the eight stories had been completed when the structure began to be noticeably uneven. The soil underneath was not stable and the foundation was not deep enough, consequently the tower sunk on one side. But during that period, war had broken out between various Italian city-states, and construction was halted for almost 100 years."

"—and that is why it's called the *leaning* tower of Pisa!" confirmed Lola.

"Indeed, Lola! You are quite right," confirmed Galileo. Then he added: "There were many unsuccessful attempts to upright the Tower over the centuries— some almost disastrous! Finally in the year 1990, a multinational task force of engineers, mathematicians and historians gathered to discuss methods to stabilize the tower. The tower was closed to the public and the bells were removed to relieve some weight. Cables were cinched around the third level and anchored hundreds of feet away. The final solution was the removal of soil from underneath the side opposite to the tilt. The efforts returned the tower to a mere 10 degree angle, and the tower was reopened to the public."

"That is great—I think it looks like a beautiful lopsided wedding cake!" exclaimed Lola. "Hopefully they will leave it alone and it will stay that way forever. Otherwise we could not call it the 'Leaning Tower of Pisa' any longer," she concluded.

"That is exactly what some citizens of Pisa say too. Not many people are fortunate to see structures such as this one. It is an experience that you won't soon forget!" added Galileo.

"Thanks for visiting us tonight," said Dad." We've really enjoyed your inspirational story. I hope someday that Lola and I can visit your wondrous city of Pisa, and see the tower for ourselves."

Marie Curie

"Be less curious about people and more curious about ideas."

Lola was feeling a bit tired and frazzled—it had been a tough day for her!

First, there was a really hard math test, then she made a mess at lunch when she dropped her yogurt, *and then* she hurt her wrist when she fell during basketball practice. Coach advised Dad to have a doctor check out the injury right away. The x-ray showed that everything was ok, but she had sprained her wrist, and would have to wear a brace while it healed. Lola was glad that her wrist wasn't broken; she would recover quickly. Now she was finally home and resting, ready for her story.

"How are you feeling?" asked Dad. "Are you ready for another chapter tonight? I found just the right person to learn about this evening: Marie Curie!"

"Really? Why did you choose her, Dad?" Lola asked.

"Because you had an x-ray this afternoon," he replied, "and Marie Curie helped develop that technology. Thanks to her studies, we were able to see right away the extent of your injury."

"Of course—now I remember! I learned about Ms. Curie from school," replied Lola. "We actually read about her in French class a few weeks ago."

"I'm so glad my work was able to assist you," said a woman's voice. Before them stood Marie Curie! She was dressed in a dark blue, mid-length dress with pouf shoulders and long sleeves. Her graying hair was pulled back into a bun, and her eyes sparkled with intelligence.

"Welcome Madam Curie!" said Lola. "Can you tell us about your work? I know that you were a physicist and a chemist, and I learned in school that you were the first woman to win a Nobel Prize...what's a Nobel Prize?"

"Well, young lady, the Nobel Prize is a set of prestigious awards named after the Swedish inventor, Alfred Nobel. The prizes are given every year by Swedish and Norwegian committees to individuals in recognition of their accomplishments and contributions in the fields of physics, chemistry, physiology or medicine, literature, peace, and economics. I received my first Nobel Prize with my husband in 1903 for our discovery of the principles of radioactivity. I was awarded my second Nobel in 1911 for chemistry. I used the prize money to continue my research."

"Were there many women scientists in your day?" asked Dad.

"Not at all!" answered Madam Curie. "I was born in Warsaw, Poland in 1867 during the Victorian era, a time when opportunities for women were few and far between. When I was a young lady, Poland was controlled by Russia, and higher education was not made available to Polish citizens. However, my parents strongly believed in education, and sent me to an illegal night school known as 'The Floating University.' The school was called 'floating' because it had to change locations continuously to avoid detection by the Russian authorities."

Wow, that must have been a real challenge, thought Lola. *I can't imagine going to school in secret.*

"I worked hard and saved my earnings so that I was able to later move to Paris, France." Madam Curie continued, "I was one of only two women accepted into the School of Science at the Sorbonne, and became the first woman to receive a doctorate degree in France. As such I became the object of much gossip, but I carried on with my research and stayed focused on my ideas and insatiable curiosity for science and nature.

"While doing research at the Sorbonne, I was introduced to a fellow scientist named Pierre Curie. We shared a laboratory, and within a year we were married. We both had a passion for science and bicycling in the country. Working together, we discovered a new element, which I named 'polonium' after my native country of Poland, then the element 'radium', and x-rays, which were later exploited for the benefit of humanity.

"Pierre and I also had a wonderful family life with our two daughters, Irene and Eve. Irene eventually became my assistant, and later earned her own Nobel Prize with her husband in 1935 for their discovery of artificial radioactivity.

"Sadly, Pierre died in 1906. He had been teaching at the Sorbonne, and I was honored when the school asked me to take over Pierre's post. Thus, I became the first female professor of the Sorbonne!"

"You have achieved so many accomplishments, Doctor Curie!" declared Dad.

"I'd like to share one more with you, if I may?" said Madam Curie. "When the First World War broke out in 1914 I was devoted to helping our soldiers. I championed the use of portable x-ray machines in the field, and these medical vehicles became known as 'little Curies.'"

"That's so cool! Thanks very much for being here this evening," said Lola. "Because of your hard work, I know my wrist is not badly injured. Also, I am a very curious person and I am glad to hear that you are too, Madam Curie."

"Thank you for your kind words Lola. Yes, curiosity about the world around you is a gift indeed, and it is how we stretch our minds and grow our knowledge."

The Sorbonne

"The Sorbonne played a significant role in your life, hasn't it, Madam Curie?" asked Lola. "What is so special about it?""

"How to explain the Sorbonne?" mused Marie Curie. To her the university was more than just a bunch of decorative buildings in Paris, France—it was so much more! She gathered her thoughts. "Well, as you know, the education I received at the university is responsible for much of my success. When the Sorbonne accepted me as a student in 1891, it opened the door to higher education for all women.

"*The Vieille Dame*, or "Old Lady", as the Sorbonne is often referred to, was one of the first Universities in the world. It was built in Paris, France in the 13th century. The school is named after Robert de Sorbon, who established the college in 1257, to teach theology to a small group of poor students, at a time when only the wealthy were educated. As you know, Lola, theology is the study of religion. The Sorbonne eventually became a major center of learning and the core of the world renowned University of Paris, housing knowledge on the subjects of culture, science, and arts that spans centuries.

"In 1469, the Sorbonne installed the first printing machine in France. Can you guess another 'first' that happened at the Sorbonne?"

Lola did not know and leaned forward, eager to hear all about it.

Dad was smiling as he said "I believe I know the answer to that question—are you referring to the Olympics, by any chance?"

"That's correct!" exclaimed Marie Curie. "Baron Pierre de Coubertin came up with the idea to revive the ancient Greek games. In 1894, the Olympic Congress was created, and held the first meetings in the auditorium of the Sorbonne University in Paris. The Congress eventually became the International Olympic Committee with delegates from France, Greece, Italy, Russia, Spain, Great Britain & Ireland, Belgium, Sweden, and the USA. The first games were held in Athens, Greece, in 1896. Paris was awarded the honor of hosting the second Olympic Games in 1900. A famous motto captures the spirit of the Olympics: "Citius, Altius, Fortius", which is Latin for "Faster, Higher, Stronger" and encourages athletes to give their best in competition. Pierre de Coubertin borrowed the phrase from his friend Henri Didon, a Dominican priest who was passionate about sports."

"Wow," said Lola, "that is *so* inspiring! What else can you tell us about this awesome place?"

"The Sorbonne has also undergone many transformations in its long history." said Madam. "In 1622, the president of the Sorbonne, Cardinal Richelieu, decided to rebuild the university. In 1635 The Sorbonne church began construction, and housed Richelieu's tomb and his sculpture. Today, the chapel is the only building remaining from this time. Cardinal Richelieu was a very important figure in both the

Catholic Church and the Government of France in the 1600s. He became Cardinal and then the chief minister to France's King Louis XIII. Richelieu was also famous for his patronage of the arts.

"The largest reconstruction began in 1885 and was completed in 1901, when it emerged as the New Sorbonne, which now has a beautiful courtyard surrounded by a row of columns, known as a 'peristyle.' The courtyard is decorated with plaques printed with all the names of all the academies in France, and shields with the coat-of-arms of all the towns with a high school in them.

"The Sorbonne Reading Room is one of the most amazing university libraries in the world. It is Europe's largest library with 470,000 books. Students studying at the library have a view of the fabulous artwork that adorns the ceiling and walls."

Pretty magnificent," thought Lola.

"Over the years," Madam Curie explained, "the Sorbonne flourished—so much, in fact, that by the late 1950s, the number of students enrolled was *ten times* greater than the number it had been built for! New buildings were added in the 1950s and 1960s to accommodate so many people.

"In 1970, the University of Paris was divided into thirteen different universities, with four of them maintaining facilities in the historical building of the Sorbonne. Today, the Sorbonne is dedicated to the studies of literature, the humanities, world languages, social sciences, civilization, and the arts."

"That's a really interesting history!" said Lola. "Thank you for telling us about this amazing place."

"And I thank you, also." said Madam Marie Curie with a gentle smile. "The *Vieille Dame* and I have something in common. We are both 'old ladies' with much to share with the world."

Rita Levi-Montalcini

"Above all, don't fear difficult moments. The best comes from them."

Lola was feeling tired and happy. Tired because her day had been busy, and happy because she was wearing a brand-new nightgown. The new sleepwear was super soft, with lots of stars on a deep blue background - just like her beloved night sky! Lola performed one last twirl in front of the mirror before settling down for her nightly reading time with Dad.

"Smart *and* stylish!" laughed Dad, as he sat next to Lola and opened their special book to a new chapter.

"And that's also me!" exclaimed a high-pitched voice. "I was known for my intellect as well as my fashion sense."

A tiny woman materialized before them—it was Dr. Rita Levi-Montalcini! Her white hair was artfully styled, her hands were beautifully manicured, and she was wearing high heels with her lab coat. This diminutive scientist exuded confidence!

"Pleased to make your acquaintance Dr. Levi-Montalcini," said Dad. He was excited to have another female Nobel Prize recipient come and talk to his daughter.

"Can you explain to Lola what it was like to study science in your time?" he asked.

"Certainly," replied their visitor. "I was born in 1909 in Turin, Italy, to a wealthy Jewish family. My father, Adamo Levi, was a gifted mathematician and electrical engineer. My mother, Adele Montalcini, was a talented artist. I had an older brother named Gino, who was an architect and professor at the University of Turin. I had two sisters: Anna, who was five years older, and Paola, my twin. Paola became well-known in Italy for her painting."

Dr. Levi-Montalcini continued, "I was raised during the Victorian era, Lola. While my parents were highly cultured and intellectual, they nevertheless felt that a woman's place was in the home. My brother was sent to university, but my father would not allow myself or my sisters to pursue studies that would lead to a career."

"Oh, so studying art was allowed but studying science wasn't?" asked Lola.

"That's right," came the reply. "I always knew that I would not thrive in the role of homemaker. When I was twenty, my father finally relented and allowed me to go to college.

"I graduated from medical school in 1936 with a summa cum laude degree in medicine and surgery. I then enrolled in a three year specialization in neurology and psychiatry—but my studies were interrupted by the beginning of the Second World War. Laws were passed barring non-Aryan Italian citizens from academic and professional careers, so I spent a short time in Brussels, Belgium, as a guest of a neurology institute before returning to Turin to join my family."

"That must have been a very difficult time for you," said Dad. "How did you manage to continue your studies during the war?"

Dr. Rita Levi-Montalcini raised her chin defiantly and winked at Lola. "I was a very stubborn scientist, and I simply could not let discrimination and war interrupt my important work! As Germany invaded Italy we were forced to adapt as best we could—but my family always stayed together. We had to move numerous times: from Turin, to the countryside, to Florence where my family had to live underground until the war ended. I used my ingenuity to build a mini-laboratory to conduct experiments in my bedroom.

"In 1944, the English-American armies forced the German invaders to leave Florence. I was hired by the military as a medical doctor to care for the war refugees. The refugee camp was flooded with epidemics of infectious diseases, including typhus. I worked tirelessly to ease their suffering.

"My family was finally able to return to Turin when the war in Italy came to an end in 1945. I happily resumed my academic positions at the University—Ah! But, my life changed again in 1947 when I was invited to America to work with Professor Viktor Hamburger at Washington University in St. Louis, Missouri. Professor Hamburger was very excited about the work I had done with nerve growth factor, a protein that promotes nerve growth in developing cells."

"Did you have a nice visit?" asked Lola.

"You could say that!" laughed the good doctor. "I intended to conduct my experiments for a few months, but the excellent results from my research led to a much extended stay in America. I partnered with a biochemist named Stanley Cohen, and our efforts resulted in a Nobel Prize in 1986 for Physiology or Medicine. Today my research is being used to help develop treatments for conditions such as Alzheimer's disease, infertility, and cancer."

"Wow! Your perseverance really paid off!" exclaimed Lola. "You really managed to overcome very difficult moments in history and accomplish great things... Thanks for all your hard work, and thanks for being here tonight to share your story."

The Human Body

Dr. Rita Levi-Montalcini was a very interesting guest. Lola had so many questions for her!

"What inspired you the most?" she asked. "I'd really like to know why you pursued your studies for so long. Did you ever get bored doing the same experiments over and over? Were you ever so discouraged that you wanted to give up? Did you ever change your mind and wish you had gotten married or started a family? Or become an artist like your mother and sister?"

"Whoa! Slow down, Lola!" exclaimed Dad. "I'm sure the doctor would appreciate one question at a time."

Their petite visitor smiled at Lola. "You remind me of myself at your age, young lady." she said. "I was always very inquisitive and I had a passion for learning. Believe me, life is never boring when you are doing what you love. Now, let *me* ask *you* a question—have you ever thought about the human body, Lola?"

"Um... not really," came the reply. "Except for when I hurt my wrist, I guess not."

"Our bodies are miraculous!" Dr. Levi-Montalcini enthused. "Consider all the intricacies of the different parts and systems that make up our human selves. Our hearts, our lungs, our bones; our senses of hearing, sight, touch, smell, and taste; our nervous system, our digestive system, just to name a few— why, the human body is so complex, it could never be boring to study!

"Let's use your wrist injury as a starting point, Lola. When you injured your wrist, were you concerned that a bone had been broken?"

"We sure were!" said Lola. "The x-ray showed that the wrist had been sprained, not broken, and we were so relieved!"

"That's because the human body is absolutely fascinating: not only beautiful and complex, but also resilient and robust. For example, did you know that your bones make up the skeletal system? The bones that sustain your body are made of one of the strongest materials found in nature. One cubic inch of bone can withstand loads of at least 19,000 pounds (8,626 kilograms), which is approximately the weight of five standard-size pickup trucks. Or that your heart pumps 60-100 times per minute, every minute, and will beat at least 2.8 billion times in the average lifespan? Can you believe that your brain makes 10 billion calculations every second in order for your eyes to see? That is as fast as the fastest supercomputers in existence today! Or that we all have an immune system which protects our body from diseases and fights the millions of germs that we are exposed to every day? In summary, the human body is so intricate, Lola, that even today we are still learning new things about this multifaceted marvel.

"We can compare the human body to a symphony, with each individual system playing a specific part. When the individual systems work together in concert, something wonderful happens! Whether it is music or life, each part contributes to the whole: our skeleton, our musculature, our heart—and our brain has the amazing ability and power to conduct and coordinate all these systems in harmony."

"Wow!" said Lola. "You make the human body sound like a work of art, Dr. Rita!"

"I truly believe that it is," replied the doctor. "However, remember also that our bodies are not indestructible, and there is only so far we can push them before they start to fail. So we shall always treat them with respect and care: good nutrition, regular exercise, and an appropriate amount of rest. Fortunately, our bodies have amazing healing capacities, too.

"My special field of study," continued Dr. Montalcini, "focused on the nervous system with the brain as the center. The brain weighs approximately three-pounds and acts as a supercomputer that runs all the systems in your body. Then, there is the spinal cord, which is a bundle of nerves that sends and returns messages to the brain from points in the body. All-in-all, the human nervous system is made of billions of nerve cells called neurons that communicate with each other through chemicals called neurotransmitters. I spent my adult life studying and experimenting with such cells. My associate, Dr. Cohen, and I worked tirelessly to isolate and identify a chemical which became known as 'nerve growth factor.' Our discovery led the way for scientists to gain a greater understanding of disorders such as cancer and Alzheimer's disease.

"You asked earlier if I might have wished to become an artist like my mother and sister. Believe it or not, Lola, but my experiments provided the perfect opportunity to combine my scientific talents with my creativity. Everything I did in the lab needed to be documented. This is an area that utilized my artistic abilities. Not only was I fascinated by my studies, but I also took great satisfaction in drawing and sketching my discoveries. So I guess you could say I had *the best of all worlds*!" she said with a smile that lit up the room.

"Dr. Rita Levi-Montalcini," said Dad "Your lifetime achievements have helped *us* have the best of all worlds. Thank you for sharing with us tonight!"

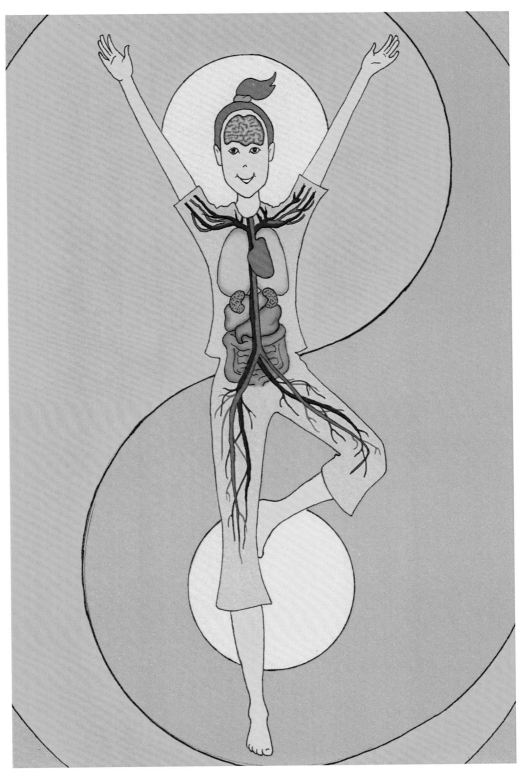

Roald Amundsen

"Victory awaits him who has everything in order..."

"What a great day," thought Lola as she got ready for bed. Her class had taken a field trip to a nature preserve, and the children were allowed to explore on their own along with a great Ranger. There were two trails to choose from, but Lola and her friends, Marlene and Idonia Mack, chose the trail less traveled— and were rewarded with the discovery of a small waterfall. It was beautiful! She and her friends had a wonderful day investigating the area around the falls. The rest of the class had chosen the easier trail, so they missed seeing Lola's extraordinary place. Lola told her Dad all about it as they prepared for their nightly ritual of reading from their special book.

As they settled down to read a new chapter, Dad flipped through the pages and showed a particular one to Lola. "I think you might have something in common with this gentleman," he said. On the page was a photograph of an older man named Roald Amundsen. Taken in the early 1920s, the sepia-colored image showed the Norwegian explorer bundled in heavy clothing with a fur trimmed hood surrounding his face—he looked very cold!

"An explorer—like you Lola! How cool is that?" asked Dad.

"Can you imagine being the *first* person to discover a new place?" wondered Lola. "I'll bet it's thrilling!"

"Thrilling *and* hard work," replied a deep voice. "Plus, meticulous planning is *essential* to success, might I add." Before them stood the arctic explorer, Roald Amundsen. He was a large man, with a weathered face and piercing eyes. He smiled at Lola and said, "I'm pleased to meet a kindred spirit, Lola! You are fortunate to have parents who support your thirst for knowledge and adventure."

"Welcome Mr. Amundsen," said Dad. "Could you tell us about the challenges you encountered in your lifetime of adventure?"

"Certainly," said Mr. Amundsen. "To begin, first let me give you some background about myself. I was born in the year 1872, in Borge, Norway. I grew up there with my three brothers; I was the youngest. My family's life revolved around the sea. Everyone was either a shipowner or a captain. I dreamt of being an explorer! However, we lost my father when I was 14, and my mother decided then and there that I would not meet the same fate. To please her, I studied to become a doctor, but my true desire was to become an explorer at sea. I followed my mother's wishes until she died when I was 21 years old. That is when I left school to pursue my dream.

"Times were different back then," he continued, "and we did not have the modern conveniences that you enjoy today, Lola. For example, in 1887 I was the first mate on a ship named the Belgica. We were the first expedition to survive the winter in the Arctic. In those days, many sailors became sick from scurvy—an illness caused by a lack of vitamin C. We didn't have your chewable multivitamins back in my day!

"It was a grueling trip, but I learned many valuable lessons on that voyage that would help me on later expeditions. Important things such as using animal skins for warmth—our wool coats were no match for the arctic weather. I also learned that we could avoid scurvy by eating fresh seal meat when citrus fruit was unavailable.

"By 1903 I commanded my own ship, the Gjøa, which is pronounced 'yu-a' in Norwegian. One of my greatest accomplishments was the discovery of the Northwest Passage from the Atlantic Ocean to the Pacific Ocean. The Northwest Passage is a sea route along the northern coast of North America, through the Canadian Arctic Archipelago and the coast of Canada. That journey lasted 3 whole years! During that time I learned Arctic survival skills from the Netsilik people, native of that Region. They showed me how to fish and hunt seal in the harsh environment. I learned how seal meat provides food, while their pelts provide protection from the elements. I learned that seal fat is used to make soap, and can be used as fuel for lamps and heat. The Netsilik people also introduced me to sled dogs. The knowledge gained on that voyage enabled me to succeed in my finest achievement."

"What do you consider your greatest accomplishment?" asked Lola. "What was your favorite adventure? Were you ever afraid?"

"There were many occasions to be fearful, my young friend, but I believed in myself. Why, without confidence and passion," he replied, "I never would have made my fateful journey that began in 1910. I originally intended to set out to reach the North Pole, but when I heard that Robert Peary and Frederick Cook had already claimed that feat—I changed direction. My crew sailed to the other end of the earth, and after much hardship I became the first person to ever set foot at the South Pole."

"That is an amazing feat!" declared Dad. "Thank you for telling us about your adventures tonight. Do you have any final words of wisdom to share with my future explorer?"

"I would like to leave you with a final thought: victory awaits him who has everything in order—luck, people call it. Defeat is certain for him who has neglected to take the necessary precautions in time; this is called bad luck. May you always have successful endeavors, my young friend. Plan well, be confident in yourself, and never give up!"

Antarctica

"How exactly *is* Antarctica Mr. Amundsen?" asked Lola. "We read a lot about it in Geography class but I would like to know about it from your personal experience." Once again, she had lots of questions that needed answers, and Roald Amundsen was a fountain of information! Lola and her dad were having a wonderful conversation with the great Norwegian explorer.

"Imagine a place with vast spaces where ice is just about everywhere all of the time," began their guest. "That's Antarctica! Most of Antarctica *is* in fact covered in ice. Antarctica is actually the fifth largest continent in the world. It derives its name from a Greek word meaning 'opposite to the north.' The Arctic Circle rings the southern part of the globe. Its size changes with the seasons—the expanding sea ice along the coast almost doubles its size during the winter months. Antarctica has about 90% of the world's ice, with almost 70% of the world's fresh water frozen there. The continent is divided into two regions, separated by the Transantarctic Mountain range. East Antarctica is close in size to Australia, and makes up about two thirds of the continent. The ice on this part of the continent averages over one mile thick. West Antarctica is composed of a series of frozen islands stretching toward the southern tip of South America."

"Is it true that Antarctica is considered a desert?" asked Dad. "With all that ice, how can that be?"

"You pose an excellent question," replied Mr. Amundsen. "Strange as it may sound, Antarctica is classified as a desert because so little moisture falls from the sky. More rain falls in the Sahara desert than in Antarctica! And unlike a desert region, the moisture doesn't soak into the ground but instead turns into snow that piles on top of itself. This, in turn, produces incredible blizzards—much like a desert sandstorm. Winds can reach up to 200 miles per hour."

Lola grew thoughtful. "It sounds like a very harsh environment... Do the seasons change? Is it ever summer in Antarctica?"

"Antarctica does have seasons, Lola, but because it lies in the southern hemisphere, the seasons are the opposite of the ones we are used to in the northern hemisphere. Summer runs from October to February and the rest of the year is basically winter. Arctic summer is not very warm, though—the average temperatures hover just above freezing. The South Pole is the coldest, windiest, and driest place on Earth. The lowest temperature in the world was recorded at the Russian Vostok station: -129 degrees Fahrenheit, or -89 degrees Celsius."

"Do any animals or people live there?" she asked. "Is it possible for any plants to grow?"

"The South Pole is too harsh an environment to sustain a native population. However, several thousand people live and work at various research facilities in the continent.

"There are no trees or bushes in Antarctica," explained Mr. Amundsen. "A combination of freezing temperatures, plus lack of moisture and sunlight prohibit plant growth. The only vegetation on the continent is composed of mosses, lichen, and algae.

"Surprisingly, there is an abundance of wildlife that has adapted to the extreme conditions. Many species of whales, seals and birds have an insulating layer of fat to protect them from the cold. Sea life includes a wide variety of fish and krill. Penguins spend most of their lives in the sea, eating fish and squid."

Roald Amundsen continued. "My favorite is the Emperor Penguin—they are truly amazing birds! While some animals, like the Humpback whale, leave Antarctica during the horrendous winter months, the Emperor Penguin lives on Antarctica year-round. The male Emperor Penguin is the only warm-blooded animal to remain on the continent during the harshest season, nesting and protecting the single egg laid by the female. For nine long weeks, the male cares for the egg while the female replenishes her body at sea. During that time, the male incubates the egg, and receives no nourishment for himself—he must rely on his store of fat. It is estimated that the male loses half his body weight by the time the females return and the eggs are hatched."

Lola laughed and hugged her father. "Those penguin guys are almost as dedicated as you, Dad!" she exclaimed.

"Right you are!" said Dad, hugging her back.

"It warms my heart to visit folks like you," said Roald. "Exploring was my passion, and I devoted my life to discovering uncharted places. I never married or had children of my own, so it is truly a pleasure to share my stories with you tonight."

"Thank you, Mr. Amundsen," replied Dad. "I'm sure that young people everywhere will be inspired by your courageous travels. Goodnight!"

44

Queen Elizabeth I

"A clear and innocent conscience fears nothing."

It was finally time for Lola and her Dad to read from their special book, and Lola couldn't wait to find out who would visit next. Every chapter brought a new and exciting guest!

"I wonder what's in store for us this evening," said Dad as he paged through the book. "If you were in charge, who would you invite next, Lola?"

"You mean, 'in charge' like a teacher or maybe... a Queen?" asked Lola. "Yes, that's it—I think I would really like to meet a Royal person tonight!" she said with a smile.

Lola flipped rapidly through the pages. Finally she stopped at the portrait of a pale young lady dressed in an elaborate brocade gown festooned with beads. The dress had lots of lace trim, with an enormous frilly collar that surrounded the face. A beautiful crown rested atop an intricate hairdo.

"Wow, Dad! Look at that outfit. She must be a Princess!" exclaimed Lola.

"A Queen, actually, my dear," responded a soft cultured voice. The voice belonged to the regal woman who had materialized before them. "Allow me to introduce myself: I am Elizabeth I, Queen of England and Ireland."

"We are pleased to meet you, your Majesty!" said Lola. "Your gown is so beautiful! Is that a real crown? Please, tell us about your life."

"Such a passionate young lady!" replied the Royal guest. "I am most happy to answer all of your questions. Yes, this is a real crown; and this gown that you admire so much? I wore this ensemble when I became Queen of England and Ireland in 1558 at the age of 25. I then reigned for 44 years and 127 days."

Elizabeth continued, "My parents were King Henry VIII and his second of six wives, Anne Boleyn. To this day, the successor to the English throne is the oldest male descendent of the reigning monarch. If there are no males, it goes to the oldest female descendent. So, when my father died in 1547, my half-brother, Edward became King. Edward died in 1553 and my half-sister, Mary took over as Queen. She died in 1558 with no children. Therefore, I was crowned to the throne of England, and became Queen Elizabeth I. Prior to that I had been called Lady Elizabeth. I never married and never had any children. For this reason, I am sometimes known as The Virgin Queen."

"Wow," commented Lola. "What was your childhood like, your Majesty?"

Queen Elizabeth I reminisced: "I was very fortunate, Lola. I was raised as a royal child, with many privileges. My governess, Kat Ashley, was appointed when I was but 4 years old. Kat taught me to speak four languages: French, Flemish, Italian, and Spanish. Other tutors also taught me to write and speak English, Latin, and Greek. By the time I became Queen, I was considered one of the best educated women of my generation. Later in life, I also learned to speak Welsh, Cornish, Scottish, and Irish. One should always keep learning, I believe."

"I agree!" said Dad. "I always try to encourage Lola with her studies. We believe it's also important to exercise, to be creative, and to keep our bodies and minds fit. What are your thoughts on the arts, your highness?"

"My dear friends, I believe that the arts are of the utmost importance!" declared the Queen. "During my reign, I was steadfast in my artistic pursuits. I loved all music, and played the lute. Writers, painters and poets flourished! I encouraged travel and exploration.

"This period is sometimes referred to as 'The Golden Age' and I am very proud the arts blossomed while I was Queen."

"Can you please tell us about England's defeat of the Spanish Armada and your secret to success?" asked Dad.

"But of course!" replied Queen Elizabeth.

"In May 1588 a fleet or 'Armada' sailed from the port of Lisbon, Spain, bound for England. At that time, England was a small nation with a little navy. The English fleet was greatly outnumbered, but our ships had the advantage of being smaller and easier to maneuver. Strategy and weather allowed the English fleet to deal a devastating blow to the Armada. The great history of the English navy began right then, as did serious English exploration and colonization."

"The secrets to my success are rooted in my beliefs," concluded the Queen. "I never hid myself away in my palace; I traveled to meet my people and see my troops on the front line. People need to know what is expected of them, while a leader needs to be aware that the people have needs and want to contribute to their destiny. Also, a leader must surround themselves with bright people. One person cannot know everything, nor can one person do everything. I learned that if you keep a clear and innocent conscience, you will always face your challenges without fear."

"Thank you for a lovely visit this evening your Majesty," saluted Lola. "You are truly one of history's great leaders!"

The Tower of London

"You have led a life of privilege," remarked Dad to Queen Elizabeth I. "Was there ever a time of hardship for you?"

Lola was surprised at her dad's question. "She was the Queen of England, Dad—with servants and jewels and tutors! That sounds like a pretty nice life to me," she said.

The Queen gently shook her head and sighed. "Lola, my dear, the life of a Royal can be fraught with uncertainty. One always had to be aware of all the court intrigue that could change your circumstances in the blink of an eye. My poor mother, Anne Boleyn, suffered such a fate. One day she was the Queen of England, married to King Henry VIII, and the next, she was a prisoner in the Tower of London before she was executed.

"I, myself, was a 'guest' of the Tower in 1554 during the reign of my half-sister Mary. Those were difficult times indeed," she said sadly.

"Wow! You were really kept prisoner in a tower? Like Rapunzel?" asked Lola.

"It is true," explained their visitor, "but the Tower of London is not quite as you imagine Lola. The Tower of London is really a combination of buildings. It is the oldest palace, fortress, and prison in Europe, with an impressive history.

"William the Conqueror began to build the complex in the early 1080s when he decided he needed a stronghold in London. The site he chose was the very same location where a Roman fortress had been built over a thousand years before. Traces of the original Roman wall are still visible even after all this time.

"The Tower was originally built as a simple stone and timber enclosure with a clear view of the Thames River. William the Conqueror wanted a fortress to keep troublemakers, misfits, and overall bad guys under control, and chose the location to be able to see any enemies approaching from the river. Since then, the Tower of London has constantly been expanded. It gradually became a complex used for many purposes by the royals. The first stone structure became known as The Great Tower. Rectangular in shape, the walls are 15 feet thick and 90 feet tall, with four turrets at the corners."

The Queen continued, "In the year 1240, King Henry III decided to make the Tower of London his home. He had the tower white-washed, expanded the grounds, and added a church, a great hall, and other buildings. The tower became known as La Tour Blanche—*The White Tower*. As more buildings were constructed around the White Tower, the complex grew, and King Henry III decided to rename the area The Tower of London. During his reign, King Henry III used the complex as a prison and royal residence, often hosting elaborate parties and entertaining guests who came with gifts of animals.

"In 1235, Emperor Frederick II gifted King Henry III three lions because they matched the three lions on the king's shield. The emperor had just married the king's sister, Isabella, so the animals were seen as a sign of friendship and allegiance between the two kingdoms. This led to the creation of the Royal Menagerie."

"Animals? Really?" asked Lola. "Why on earth would anyone give the king an animal as a gift?"

"The world was very different back then, Lola," explained the Queen. "Travel was quite primitive, with much of the world still to be discovered. In those days, powerful rulers tried to impress and out-do each other by exchanging 'living gifts' of exotic animals. Sadly, most of the animals did not flourish in their new home. First, they had to survive the journey to London, and because they had never been seen in that part of the world before, the menagerie keepers didn't know how to take care of them once they arrived. Animal care at the Tower of London was mostly trial and error, as the animals were kept in unsuitable, cramped quarters and fed food that was not part of their natural diet. The menagerie grew to become a very popular excursion for the people of London. Where else could the common folk see the exotic creatures they had only heard about before?

"Besides the much improved menagerie, today the Tower of London houses the Crown Jewels and has done so for many centuries now. The estimated value of the crown jewels is said to exceed 32 billion dollars but their actual value is priceless. Also, at the tower one can see the royal ravens (at least six at any given time). The ravens have their wings clipped to prevent them from flying away. Legend has it that when there are no longer ravens in the Tower of London the Commonwealth of England will fall.

"Many walls and smaller towers were added over the years, all enclosed within a moat that receives its water from the Thames. It has changed a great deal from my time! Today the official title of the tower is Her Majesty's Royal Palace and Fortress, though it is commonly referred to as the Tower of London."

"What about the Beefeaters we hear about, who are they?" enquired Lola.

"The Beefeaters, also known as Yeoman Warders," promptly replied Queen Elisabeth, "are guardians of the Tower of London who live on site at the tower. In principle, they are responsible for protecting the British crown jewels, but in practice they are tour guides."

"That's quite a history, your majesty!" said Lola. "Thank you for telling us about this amazing place!"

Socrates

"The unexamined life is not worth living."

"You look thoughtful this evening," said Dad as he strolled into Lola's room with their special book in hand. "Is everything alright?"

Lola was sitting cross legged in the big comfy armchair with her chin in her hands. "I've just been wondering about something, Dad...what exactly is a *paradox*? I'm confused!"

"Oh, I see. Hmmm, how best to describe a paradox..." he mused. Dad settled next to Lola and opened the big book. "I think the person in this next chapter just might be able to help us figure that out, Lola."

"Most assuredly!" replied a strong, gravelly voice. The gentleman who appeared before them wore the draped robes of ancient Greece. Short in stature, the newly arrived guest sported a full beard and mustache, and long, unkempt hair. His bulging eyes glowed with intensity. Lola recognized him instantly! He looked just like his picture that was on display in the school library.

"Good evening, Mr. Socrates," she said. "It's nice to meet you."

"The pleasure is all mine," replied their visitor. "I am known simply as Socrates, and I will be delighted to answer your thoughtful question in a moment. First, let me tell you a little about myself.

"I was born many, many years ago—around 470 BCE in Athens, Greece. My father was a stone mason named Sophroniscus, and my mother, Phaenarete, was a midwife. Although my family was not wealthy, I was given a good basic Greek education before following in my father's footsteps as a stone mason.

"I was married to Xanthippe, who was much younger than me. We had three sons named Lamprocles, Sophroniscus, and Menexenus.

Socrates continued, "In ancient Athens, all able-bodied men were required to serve as 'citizen soldiers' from the time they turned 18 until age 60. Whenever we were needed, men of my station joined with our regular army to protect our city. Athens was at war many times in my day, so I was honor-bound to serve in the armored infantry. My military unit was known as the 'hoplite'— we wore face masks and carried shields and long spears. I fought in three large battles, and earned a reputation for my courage and fearless fighting."

"I didn't realize you had been a stone mason or a soldier," commented Dad. "I always thought you were a philosopher, sir."

"A philosopher?" asked Lola. "What kind of job is that?"

Socrates smiled as he answered, "By definition, a philosopher is a person, any person who loves wisdom. Someone who asks questions, Lola. I believed it was important to examine human nature, to explore why people behave as they do and make the choices they do, to create dialog among those of differing opinions. I felt it was very important that we learn about ourselves, to find out how we conduct ourselves and behave with others and the world around us.

"I never professed to have answers. You see, after my battle experiences, I had so many questions regarding mankind's behavior. I ventured everywhere in the city of Athens, posing my questions to all who would listen. Together, we learned how to think a problem through, then discuss it with the objective of arriving at a reasonable conclusion. Today, that process is known as the Socratic Method. In fact, I believe that only if you take a good look at your life and thoroughly examine each aspect of it by constantly asking yourself questions about your actions and choices, you lead a life worth living. That is why I came up with the expression *the unexamined life is not worth living.* Over time, I gathered many students with whom I shared ideas. One of my most ardent followers was named Plato. We had so many thought-provoking discussions that Plato decided to write everything down—he didn't want to forget what had been learned. Thankfully, Plato's writings endured through the centuries to help future generations learn of my theories.

"Now, it's time to address *your* important question, young lady," said Socrates. "'What is a paradox,' you ask? Simply put, a paradox is a statement that contradicts itself because it contains two statements that are both true but cannot be true at the same time. For example, now-a-days you say: 'Bittersweet' or 'I am nobody' or 'Wise fool'. You can be either *wise* or *a fool* but in general you cannot be wise *and* a fool at the same time."

"Oh! I get it now!" exclaimed Lola. "Before you arrived, I was thinking about your quote 'I know that I know nothing', which I saw written on a poster at school this morning as an example of a 'paradox'... I didn't understand what it meant, but now I do—in order for a person to start learning, they have to first acknowledge the fact that *they know nothing*. This awareness is the first step towards learning. Wow! That is a very bold statement, if I ever heard one!"

Socrates beamed with pride—here was another student on the path he had worked so hard to forge!

"Indeed, Lola. Now you are beginning to understand the 'love of wisdom.'"

Dad reached out to shake hands with Socrates. "Thank you, sir, for sharing your insights with us this evening," he said. "I know this is one visit that will inspire us every day!"

Athens

Lola thought Socrates was a delightful guest. He spoke so eloquently!

Dad thought so, too. "I'm curious about your home life—what can you tell us about ancient Athens, sir?"

"Athens was the greatest city-state in all of ancient Greece!" declared Socrates. "Greece is a country in Europe, overlooking the Mediterranean Sea. The main part of Greece is on a peninsula, a body of land surrounded on three sides by water. The rest of the country is made up of many islands, which made it difficult to unite as one autonomous country. So, the Greeks began to build city-states that each had their own rulers, laws, and currency. Most of the city-states had a couple thousand citizens, or fewer.

"In early 500 BCE the people of Athens decided to rule themselves, instead of having a king or queen. They created the first democracy in history, where the city was ruled by the people—but not *all* the people. There were at least 30,000 citizens when democracy began in Athens, but only men could have a say in how the city was run. Women, slaves, and foreigners could not vote. A Council was created, with at least 500 members, all men, chosen for one year positions. As many as 5,000 citizens would meet every ten days on a hill known as Pnyx. The stones of this historic meeting place are still visible in Athens today.

"A man by the name of Pericles was the leader of the new democracy. He had many buildings constructed, such as the Parthenon and the Temple of Athena Nike, two of the many buildings that made the Acropolis. The remains are of great importance in the life of the citizens of Athens.

"Acropolis is Greek for *upper city*," explained their guest. It is a citadel, or fortress, located on a rocky hill above the city of Athens. The city is named after the goddess Athena, daughter of the most powerful god, Zeus. The Parthenon is a temple dedicated to Athena. She was known for her wisdom, kindness, and compassion. Athena was also one of the 12 most powerful ancient Greek gods. She lived on Mount Olympus, the home of the Greek gods. The Olympic Games of today derive their name from the stadium of Olympia, at the base of Mount Olympus."

Socrates continued, "The largest city in Greece, Athens is considered to be one of the world's oldest cities. Built approximately 3,400 years ago it is often referred to as 'the cradle of Western civilization.' This is because it was the first city to lay down the foundations of today's civilized Western people and countries. Athens contributed to art, literature, science, and philosophy—and, in fact, to most all intellectual endeavors!

"The city-state of Athens placed great importance on education. The city was famous for having the best literature, poetry, drama and schools. Sons of nobles received higher education in science, art, politics, and government. I became known throughout the city for my teaching of philosophy.

"We just talked about what a philosopher is and how he tries to explain the nature of life with many questions," clarified Socrates. "In fact, I believe that we all have a philosopher inside, particularly kids. My dear, how many times have you asked the question 'Why?'" Dad and Lola looked at each other with a smile. "How many times have you wondered how far does the sky go? How was the universe created? Why do we have wars? What is the reason I came to Earth? Why can't we know what will happen tomorrow? Why, why, why... Big and small, these are all philosophical questions. They take us through a journey of discovery and the more questions we ask and the more curious the questioner, the bigger the world around us appears."

Socrates continued, "I taught by asking questions, and encouraged my students to 'know thyself' and to 'question everything.' We spoke about Plato, another famous Athenian and a student of mine who started a school called The Academy. And, of course, there was Aristotle. He is responsible for introducing logic, the scientific method, and the *golden mean*: everything in moderation. They were great individuals who truly inspired the rest of the world for civilizations to come, all the way to our times!"

"Wow," said Lola. "Athens sounds like one of the most incredible, and amazing places ever! Thank you for joining us this evening and *thank you* for reminding me how important it is to always be curious about life and our surroundings and to never be afraid to ask questions. As kids it is very important to hear it from individuals of your character, as well as teachers and parents. This way we shall never stop learning. I'll dream of visiting this wondrous city for many nights to come!"

William Shakespeare

"Love all, trust a few, do wrong to none."

Lola sighed contentedly. It was her favorite time of day. She sat on her favorite chair and settled in for the nightly ritual of reading with her Dad. The special book they brought home from the flea market was truly a treasure!

"How was your day, Lola?" asked Dad as he sat down next to her. He opened the book to a random page. "Is there anything you'd like to share before we begin reading?"

"There's a new poster in the school hall today," replied Lola. "I really like it. There is a quote by William Shakespeare that says, 'This above all: to thine own self be true.' Isn't that beautiful? I wish I could write like that!" she said.

"Perhaps one day you shall," responded a deep, sonorous voice. Another guest had arrived!

Lola looked across the room and saw what appeared to be a middle-aged gentleman, dressed in 15th century clothing. His hair was long, but missing from the top, giving the impression of a very high forehead. He sported a mustache and goatee, and his eyes twinkled with merriment. Their visitor was none other than the Bard of Avon, the greatest writer in the English language: William Shakespeare!

Shakespeare bowed to Lola. "You appear to be a young lady of superior intellect. I am certain that if you apply yourself, you too will write many memorable words of beauty."

"Welcome, Mr. Shakespeare!" said Dad. "It is an honor to have you here with us tonight. Lola and I are great admirers of your work. We recently saw a production of your comedy *A Midsummer Night's Dream* and we both really enjoyed the performance."

"We sure did! Have you written a lot of plays, Mr. Shakespeare?" asked Lola. "How about poetry? Did you write other things besides comedy theatre? Did you ever perform any of your own works? Were you famous in your lifetime? I'd like to learn all about you, sir."

"All very good questions," replied Shakespeare. "My story begins in Stratford-upon-Avon, England, at the very end of the Middle Ages. My birth wasn't noted in official documents, but my Baptism at Holy Trinity Church was recorded as April 26th, 1564. My father was a leather merchant and my mother was a landed heiress. I had two older sisters and three younger brothers. We had a boisterous household!

"I married Anne Hathaway in 1582, when she was 26 and I was 18. Shortly after, our daughter, Susanna was born. Our twins, Hamnet and Judith, joined our family two years later. For most of our married life, I lived in London to pursue my career while Anne raised the children in Stratford-upon-Avon. I would return once a year during Lent to see my family, and came home to Stratford permanently when I retired from theatre in 1613."

"What kind of job did you have in London?" enquired Lola.

"I worked as an actor, writer and shareholder of a London playing company known as the Lord Chamberlain's Men. By the late 1590s I became a managing partner in the company. Theatre life was a challenging career financially, Lola. In my time, theatre was considered a less than noble calling, so it was important for our company to cultivate theatre patrons among the royalty. That is why we changed the name to the King's Men in 1603—to honor King James I and gain favor in the court.

"In summer we performed at the open-air Globe Theatre, and in winter we performed indoors at the Blackfriars Theatre. Most of my early work consisted of comedies and histories for the stage. One of the lighthearted comedies was the play you admired, along with *Merchant of Venice, Much Ado About Nothing,* and *As You Like It,* to name a few. *Richard II* and *Henry VI* are two of my historic plays that dramatized weak and corrupt rulers.

"Later in my life I penned many tragedies that resonated with the public. Perhaps you are familiar with *Macbeth, Othello, King Lear* and *Hamlet*? Each of those stories explores moral failures in the hero, often bringing destruction and loss."

Shakespeare concluded, "Truth be told, young Lola, writing was my true love—my passion in life! I wrote over 35 plays, 154 sonnets and two narrative poems. My efforts have resulted in my work being performed more often than any other playwright! I worked very hard to achieve that status. But I never allowed myself to give up. I hope you will continue to follow your dreams, my young friend."

"You certainly are an inspiration for young people, Mr. Shakespeare!" said Dad. "Thank you for sharing your story with us this evening."

"All's well that ends well!" quipped The Bard.

The Human Imagination

"You have written an amazing 37 plays and 154 sonnets, Mr. Shakespeare," said Lola. "Wherever did you find all those ideas for your stories? What inspired you to write in the first place?"

"Why, my imagination, of course!" replied Shakespeare. "Our minds possess the ability to create and form new ideas, images and concepts, Lola. All anyone needs is the desire and determination—and the stories will flow!

"Story-telling is as old as time," continued the Bard. "Every culture throughout the ages has utilized storytelling to convey ideas, to teach morals and values, to share history. Oral storytelling existed long before the written word. By adding gestures and facial expressions, a storyteller could transform their important information into a source of entertainment, much like my plays!

"There are different types of stories, many of which originated to convey a lesson. Fairy tales are a good example. Are you familiar with any stories that begin 'Once upon a time'?"

"Oh yes!" replied Lola. "I love magical stories about dragons and castles and heroes!"

"Indeed?" laughed their guest. "You are in good company, then. Fairy tales almost always have a happy ending, which makes them very popular. The stories usually have a lesson, or moral teaching, and are frequently quite entertaining."

"I'm sure many stories were embellished with retelling," commented Dad wryly.

"Very true, very true!" agreed Shakespeare. "But, those embellishments kept the stories from becoming boring for those already familiar with the tale.

"Another type of story is the legend, which is often about a person who may, or may not, have actually existed. The situations in the narrative are just 'real' enough to the imaginative listener to be believable. The legend of King Arthur and the Knights of the Round Table is a perfect example. King Arthur is a medieval figure who was the king of Camelot in the 5th century. It has been suggested that King Arthur may have been a military leader that led the British forces to victory against the Saxons. Arthur's adventures were shared orally for generations before being written down as a poem in the late 1400s. The legend of King Arthur has been transformed over the years into a complex, intriguing story."

"Hmmm… so, imagination is the key to good storytelling?" asked Lola thoughtfully, "Which leads to dreaming and creating… I think I get it now! My favorite subject in school is science. After spending time with Galileo and Sally Ride, I was really inspired to learn more about our world and space exploration. But after listening to you, Mr. Shakespeare, I now realize that if

I apply my imagination with my science knowledge—I could actually create something new, with no limit to what I can create and share. I'm so excited!"

Shakespeare was very pleased at Lola's enthusiasm.

"I believe my work here is done!" he announced. With a smile and a bow, the Bard faded as silently as he had arrived.

Dad gently closed the book. He and Lola sat together peacefully for a few moments, both lost in thought.

Lola sighed, "I can't believe that was the last chapter, Dad. I'm really going to miss our special guests!"

"Me, too. We certainly learned a lot from this book haven't we? I suspect the lady from the flea market knew just what she was doing when she presented you with this book, Lola."

Lola smiled and hugged her dad.

"Thanks for taking the time to read with me every night—I really like spending our evenings together. This book is extra special, Dad! Each of our guests, truly brilliant minds, taught me something important. Mozart, Marie Curie, Roald Amundsen, and Shakespeare. Galileo and Sally Ride. Queen Elizabeth, Socrates, and Rita Levi-Montalcini. They also introduced me to amazingly beautiful places that will stay with me forever. They are all such incredible people who overcame all obstacles to achieve their goals, and always displayed profound appreciation and respect for themselves, others, and the world around them. I, too, will continue to be very appreciative of all I have and all that people do for me. I will do my best to pay it forward every chance I have. I have always been confident in myself, Dad, but now I truly know that I can do anything—anything at all!—if I apply myself, and never give up. If I can dream it, I can do it!"

"I am so glad to see how much you have taken from our reading adventure Lola. And, I believe in you, too, Lola" said Dad. "I can't wait to see where your dreams will take you!"

Dad paused to look into Lola's eyes.

"So, young lady, what do you plan to do with the special book now that we've reached the end?"

"Well..." she said with a smile, "I think I know just the right person to pass this book onto, Dad."

***And now that you've reached the end, dear reader,
who will you share this special book with?***

ABOUT THE AUTHOR

The author of a collection of poems, ***Of Rainbows and Stars***, and the short story collections, **Of Backpacks and Adventures**, **Upon a Reading Night** and **Upon a Reading Night 2**, Roberto Noce is a father with over two decades of corporate and entrepreneurial experience spanning the globe. He is fluent in English, Italian, and Spanish. Born in Italy, Roberto holds degrees from the University of Notre Dame, Texas A&M University, and the University of Houston. Roberto currently lives in Fulshear, Texas with his family. He is an avid cook, sailor, and tennis player.